D1149338

SWANSEA LIBRARIES
Swansea Libraries
0001253039

# A Miracle for David

## Patron Saint of Wales

Steffan Lloyd

Illustrations by Brett Breckon

Pont

Dewi Sant, or Saint David, is the patron saint of Wales. On the first day of March each year, Welsh people all over the world celebrate his special day.

Although not much is known about some saints, we know quite a lot about Dewi. He was born and grew up near the Pembrokeshire coast and spent most of his life caring for the people of Wales.

This story begins when Dewi was still a young monk. He travelled all over the country, just as his teacher Paulinus did before him, taking the word of God to remote villages and settlements. He loved to see the faces of the children as they heard about Jesus for the very first time.

Wales is a land of mountains and valleys which even today create a challenge for road builders. Imagine what it was like in Dewi's time when travelling from east to west and north to south took days instead of hours. Without proper pathways and bridges the monks often struggled against the difficult terrain. They didn't have much protection from the weather either. Their coarse woollen habits were good at keeping the water out to start with, but on a long journey their rain-soaked tunics rubbed painfully against the monks' skin.

In spite of all of the difficulties, though, Dewi and his companions enjoyed their work very much.

It wasn't always cold of course. There were beautiful days too when the sun shone. Dewi loved to watch the seasons change. In high summer the countryside was fragrant with wild flowers, and the sound of crickets and bees filled the air.

There wasn't time to stop and enjoy the view though. A long journey could be thirsty work and the monks had to carry water with them. Streams which burst their banks in winter dwindled to nothing in the summertime.

Rain or shine, the monks continued their journey, knowing that people were waiting eagerly for them. Dewi and his companions sometimes sang as they walked; it helped to keep up their spirits when the sun burned down on their heads and when their feet were sore and dusty.

People would come from far and near to listen to Dewi. At that time not everyone had heard about Jesus. Monks like Dewi were eager that everybody should understand his message of love.

There were no hospitals in those days and the sick and the lame would come and listen to Dewi in the hope that they might be cured. People knew that he had healed his blind teacher, Paulinus, through prayer, and hoped that he would be able to help them too. They also knew that he was an excellent preacher and would tell them wonderful stories from the Bible. It wasn't long before Dewi was ready to set up a monastery of his own so that other people could help with the work.

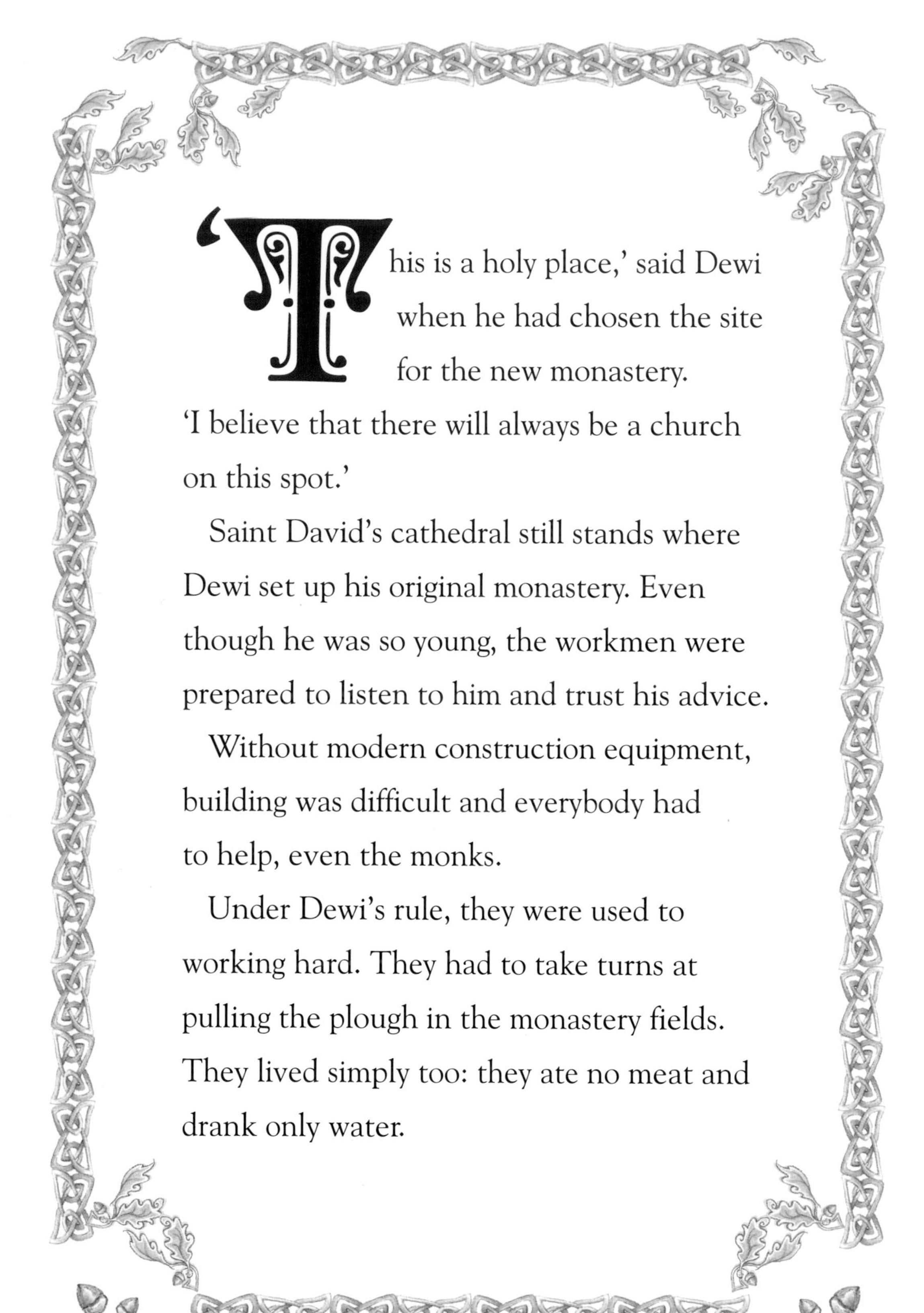

'This is a holy place,' said Dewi when he had chosen the site for the new monastery. 'I believe that there will always be a church on this spot.'

Saint David's cathedral still stands where Dewi set up his original monastery. Even though he was so young, the workmen were prepared to listen to him and trust his advice.

Without modern construction equipment, building was difficult and everybody had to help, even the monks.

Under Dewi's rule, they were used to working hard. They had to take turns at pulling the plough in the monastery fields. They lived simply too: they ate no meat and drank only water.

Llanddewibrefi

Sometimes Dewi had to leave the monastery on important business. One day, he had to go on a special journey to Llanddewi Brefi. An important meeting, or synod, was going to be held there.

A synod is a gathering of senior church-people like bishops and archbishops. They talk about important subjects and make decisions about what church members should say and do. In Dewi's time there were lots of arguments about what people should believe. A synod was where these disputes could be settled.

Synods are still held today, and church leaders, including those in Wales, still hold strong opinions about the way the church should be run.

It happened so long ago that nobody now remembers what the synod at Llanddewi Brefi was about. Some people think it was to discuss the beliefs of a teacher called Pelagius.

All we know is that Dewi was still very young when he went to the synod, even though he was already an abbot, and head of an important monastery.

Perhaps he knew he was going to have to speak in front of a lot of powerful churchmen, including Paulinus, his old teacher. All people, even saints, get nervous sometimes and we can imagine how Dewi felt!

It was a hot day for his journey and, by the end of it, Dewi was totally exhausted. He fell to the ground, not sure if he was going to be able to get up again.

From far and near the people came. Some were ordinary folk who had heard that Dewi Sant was coming to their district. They travelled on foot, laughing and chatting as they walked. For them it was a bit like being on holiday. 'I'm really excited,' said Rhiannon to her brother. 'They say that Dewi's not much older than us!'

For others the synod was important business. At that time there were no newspapers, televisions or computers, and there was certainly no internet. Chieftains and princes needed to find out about any changes which were likely to affect the way they lived. They came to the synod on horseback, riding long distances to reach such an important meeting.

'I wonder who we'll see,' said Rhiannon.

Rhiannon and her brother joined the crowd, which was starting to fill the open space outside the village. It was going to be a very, very big event.

Amongst the people were church officials, bishops and abbots, priests and monks. One of the most important of these was Paulinus, the same Paulinus whose blindness Dewi had cured. He knew the young man well. He had been abbot in the monastery where Dewi attended school and was very fond of his old pupil. He was looking forward to hearing what Dewi had to say.

Imagine how sorry Paulinus was when he saw Dewi lying on the ground. What if he wasn't well enough to address the congregation?

At last everyone had arrived but still Dewi didn't move. Paulinus spoke to him, urging him to get to his feet. He knew that Dewi's words would have a big influence on what the synod decided. He was also worried that the ordinary folk in the crowd were going to be angry if Dewi didn't speak.

'What if my voice isn't strong enough?' Dewi asked.

'Don't worry. God will give you strength,' said Paulinus. 'Come on now, Dewi!' Suddenly they were like teacher and pupil once again.

Dewi didn't want to disappoint anybody, especially Paulinus. Even though he was feeling very weak, he knew that he must get up and talk to the congregation.

Dewi rose to his feet and started to address the people. But his voice was lost in the general hubbub. Only those closest to him knew that he had begun to speak.

The people at the back of the crowd were still talking and laughing. The ground was completely flat and they couldn't even see Dewi.

'It's no good,' he said. 'My voice isn't strong. And I'm not tall enough either.'

Suddenly someone called for silence and everything went quiet. Dewi began again.

But the crowd was vast and, without seeing his face, the people at the back couldn't hear a word.

'We need a miracle,' they said.

Suddenly Dewi knew what he had to do. It was as if in the heat and in his exhaustion he had forgotten the importance of listening to God.

'How could I have forgotten?' he thought to himself. After all, that was the whole purpose of his life as a monk. Back at the monastery there were set prayers throughout the day when the monks met together in the chapel. But prayers were said at other times too, at mealtimes and even when the monks were busy at their work in the fields. Praying was as normal as eating, sleeping and breathing.

Dewi took a small white cloth from his satchel, the special bag he carried with him on his travels. He spread it on the ground, knelt down and said a prayer.

When Dewi stood up once again, the ground rose beneath his feet, and suddenly everybody could see him as he towered above the congregation.

He began to speak. His voice was strong and his face shone. The people listened, spellbound. Even those who had heard Dewi before were amazed. Never had he sounded so powerful; never were his words so wise.

Even the important churchmen were astonished at how well Dewi explained and taught. 'He has the wisdom of someone twice his age,' said one of the bishops. 'I will remember this day for ever.'

And even today, whenever people talk about Dewi Sant, they remember the miracle at Llanddewi Brefi.

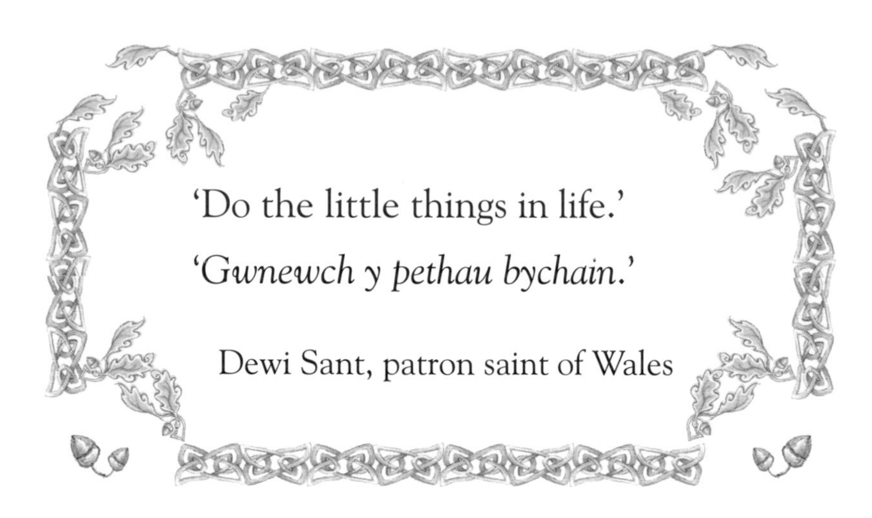

'Do the little things in life.'

*'Gwnewch y pethau bychain.'*

Dewi Sant, patron saint of Wales

First published in Wales in 2011 by Pont Books, an imprint of
Gomer Press, Llandysul, Ceredigion, SA44 4JL

ISBN 978 1 84851 165 1

A CIP record for this title is available from the British Library.



This book is published with the financial support of the
Welsh Books Council.

Printed and bound in Wales at Gomer Press,
Llandysul, Ceredigion